This edition published by Parragon Books Ltd in 2014

Parragon Books Ltd
Chartist House
15–17 Trim Street
Bath BA1 1HA, UK
www.parragon.com

ISBN 978-1-4723-3929-4

Printed in China

"It can do all the dangerous stuff while we stay safe," said Donatello.

"So it's for wimps," Raphael replied.

"Try it," Donatello said. "Attack."

Raph, Leo and Mikey all attacked, but they couldn't even make a dent!

"Let's call it Metalhead!" said Mikey.

It was now dark outside, so Michelangelo, Raphael and Leonardo went out into the city. They leaped across rooftops and waited on a ledge.

CLANG! CLANG! CLANG! Metalhead slowly caught up with them. Donatello was back in the lair, controlling the robot like a video game.

April caught up with the Turtles on her way back from the warehouse district.

"We have to do something," she said. "The Kraang are going to poison the city's water supply with mutagen!"

She quickly led the Turtles and Metalhead back to where she had come from.

Outside the warehouse, April and Metalhead waited behind while Leo, Mikey and Raph sneaked up on the Kraang.

The Turtles lurked in the dark, watching the Kraangdroids load mutagen onto trucks.

Then, on Leo's command, the three Turtles ran inside the warehouse and attacked!

"Hi-yah!" Raphael shouted.

Meanwhile, April and Metalhead watched the warehouse from outside. Just then, an energy blast shot through the roof! They heard Michelangelo shout: "They're everywhere! Run! Run!"

It sounded like the three Turtles had been cornered by the Kraang. Donnie, who was watching the action through Metalhead's eyes, knew he had to help!

Inside the warehouse, Metalhead suddenly came crashing down through the roof. The Turtles and the Kraang all stared.

"Why are you standing like that?" Leonardo asked. Metalhead's arms were in a weird position.

"Don't I look heroic?" Metalhead said in Donatello's voice.

"No!" Leonardo shouted.

"Sorry," Metalhead said. "Wrong button!"

The battle continued. Metalhead really did seem invincible! Donatello watched from the lair, excited. He made Metalhead move faster and faster, blasting lasers all over the place. Finally, he found his target.

BOOM! The mutagen exploded.

The city's water supply was safe, but Metalhead was damaged in the explosion. Donatello lost contact with the robot.

"Guys, if you can hear me, run!" Donnie shouted.

Suddenly, one Kraang brain jumped out of its damaged robot and onto Metalhead. Metalhead's eyes glowed red. Now the Kraang was controlling him! Evil Metalhead attacked the Turtles.

Donatello grabbed his bo staff and ran straight to the warehouse. He took on Evil Metalhead while the other Turtles fought the Kraang. Donnie dodged attack after attack from his own robot, until one powerful blast broke his staff in half.

"Not again!" Donnie shouted.

But then, he spotted a loose beam on the ceiling....

"Come and get me!" Donnie called out to Evil Metalhead.

Evil Metalhead sent out another laser blast. At the last second, Donnie jumped aside and the laser hit the loose beam. As it came crashing down, it fell onto the robot! Gears crunched and sparks crackled. Donnie used his broken staff to finish Evil Metalhead off. The robot was defeated! The Kraang brain jumped out and scurried away.

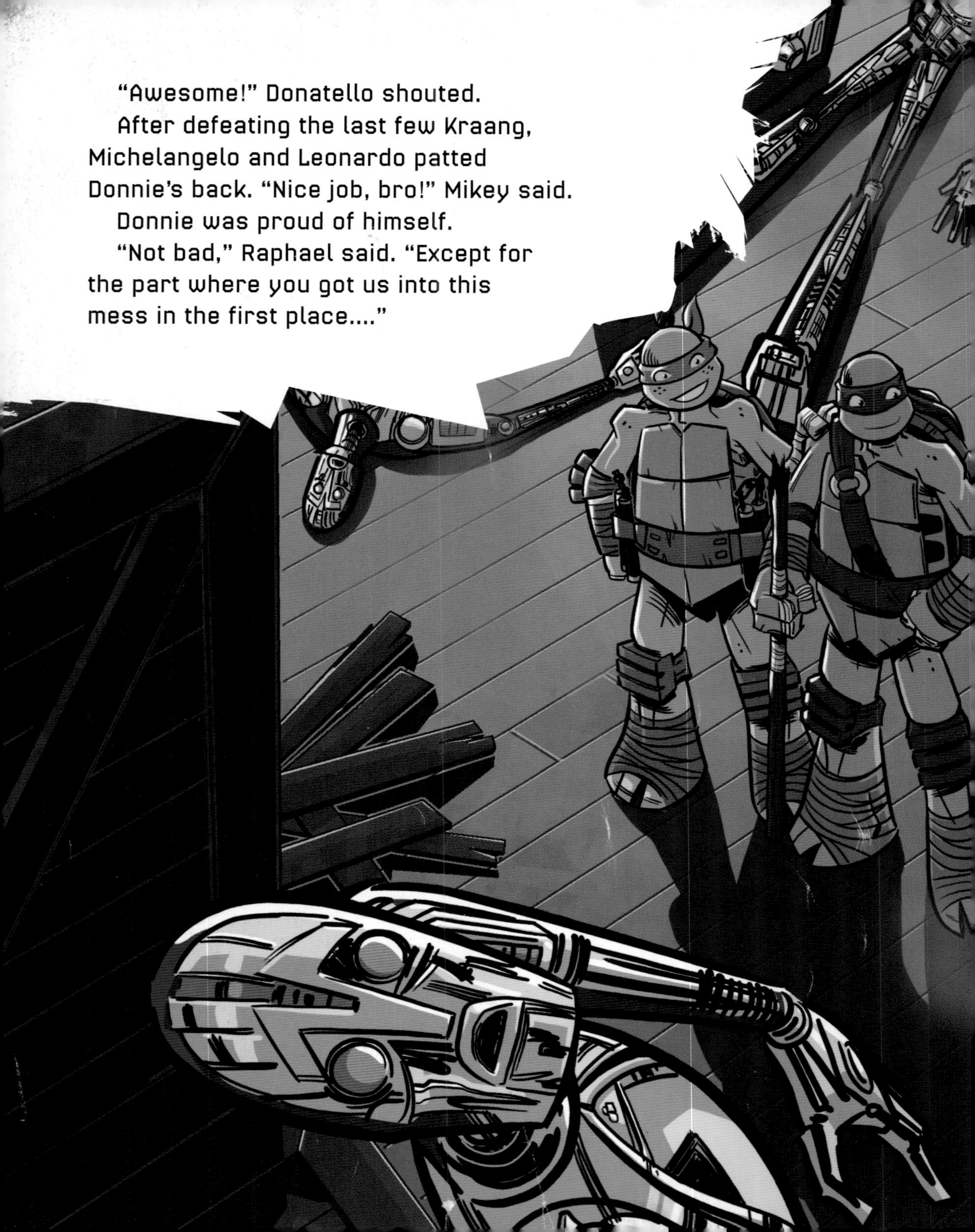

"Awesome!" Donatello shouted.

After defeating the last few Kraang, Michelangelo and Leonardo patted Donnie's back. "Nice job, bro!" Mikey said.

Donnie was proud of himself.

"Not bad," Raphael said. "Except for the part where you got us into this mess in the first place...."

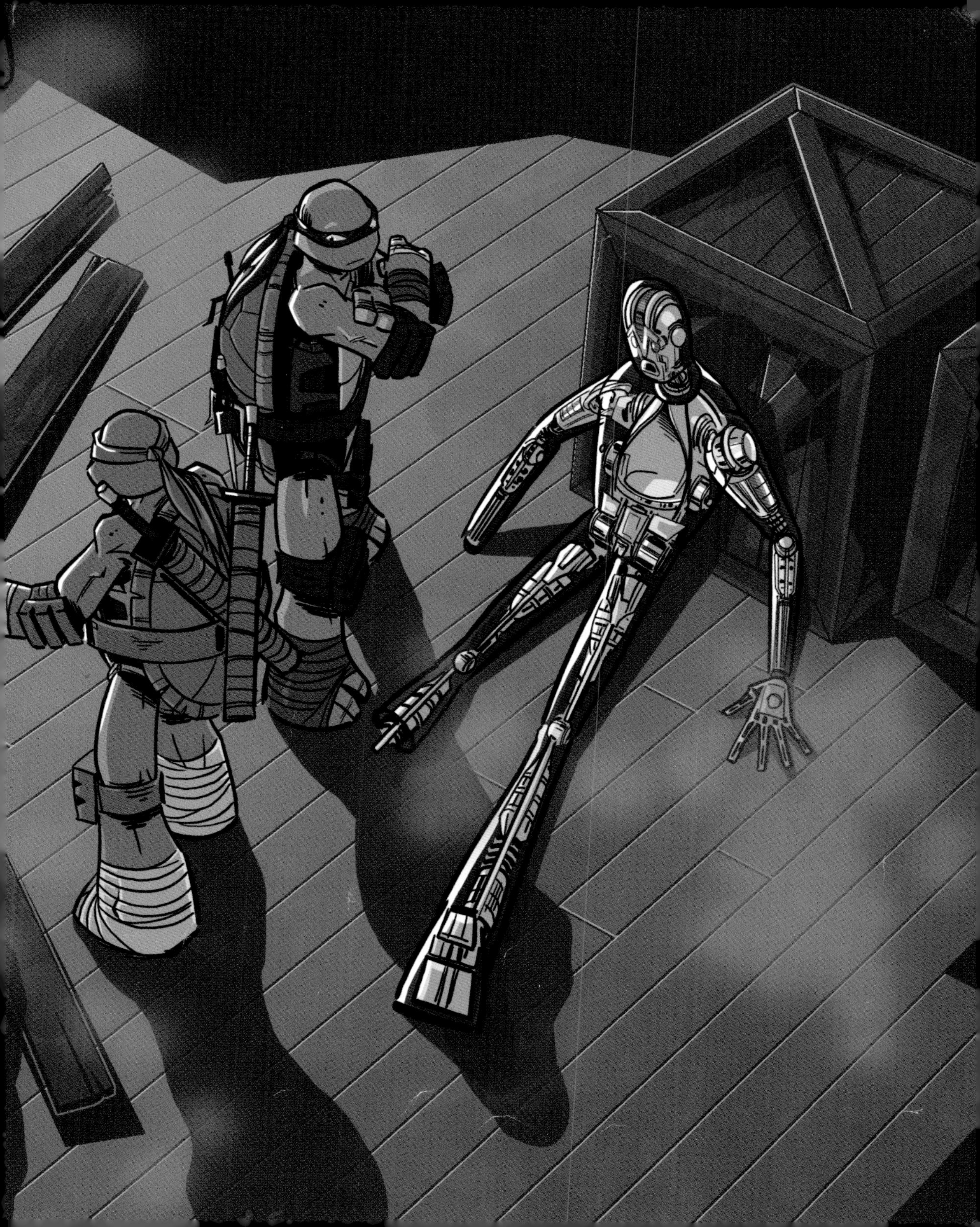

Later, back in the lair, Donatello began to work on a new project. Splinter thought he looked sad.
"What troubles you?" Splinter asked.
"This was all my fault," Donatello said.
"Yes, you are responsible," Splinter replied. "But you are also responsible for saving the city."

Donatello felt better. "In the end," he said, "there was nothing better than a wooden stick...."

"Except a laser-guided wooden stick!"

Donatello held up the new weapon he was working on – a bo staff with a laser!

But then he slammed the new bo staff on the ground and it started to make a strange sound....

"It's not supposed to do that!" Donatello cried. "RUN!"